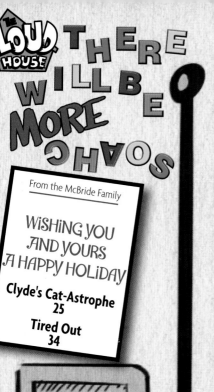

THE LOUD HOUSE
THERE WILL BE MORE CHAOS

From the McBride Family

WISHING YOU AND YOURS A HAPPY HOLIDAY

Meet the Loud Family
5

INTRODUCTION BY CHRIS SAVINO   8

nickelodeon™

#2 "THERE WILL BE MORE CHAOS"

CHRIS SAVINO – Cover Artist
JAMES SALERNO – Sr. Art Director/Nickelodeon
SEAN GANTKA–Speial Thanks
DAWN GUZZO – Design
JEFF WHITMAN – Editor
JOAN HILTY – Comics Editor/Nickelodeon
JIM SALICRUP
Editor-in-Chief

ISBN: 978-1-62991-824-2 paperback edition
ISBN: 978-1-62991-825-9 hardcover edition

Printed in China
November 2017

Distributed by Macmillan
First Printing

MEET THE LOUD FAMILY

and friends!

LINCOLN LOUD
THE MIDDLE CHILD (11)

At 11 years old, Lincoln is the middle child, with five older sisters and five younger sisters. He has learned that surviving the Loud household means staying a step ahead. He's the man with a plan, always coming up with a way to get what he wants or deal with a problem, even if things inevitably go wrong. Being the only boy comes with some perks. Lincoln gets his own room – even if it's just a converted linen closet. On the other hand, being the only boy also means he sometimes gets a little too much attention from his sisters. They mother him, tease him, and use him as the occasional lab rat or fashion show participant. Lincoln's sisters may drive him crazy, but he loves them and is always willing to help out if they need him.

LENI LOUD
THE FASHIONISTA (16)

Leni is the ditsiest of the Loud sisters. She spends most of her time designing outfits and accessorizing (though she probably can't spell the word). She is easily distracted by shiny objects, always falls for Luan's pranks, and sometimes walks into walls when she's talking (she's not great at doing two things at once). Leni might be flighty, but she's the sweetest of the Loud siblings and truly has a heart of gold (even though she's pretty sure it's a heart of blood).

LORI LOUD
THE OLDEST (17)

As the first-born child of the Loud clan, Lori sees herself as the boss of all her siblings. She feels she's paved the way for them and deserves extra respect. Her signature traits are rolling her eyes, texting her boyfriend Bobby, and literally saying "literally" all the time. Because she's the oldest and most experienced sibling, Lori can be a great ally, so it pays to stay on her good side.

LUNA LOUD
THE ROCK STAR (15)

Luna is loud, boisterous and freewheeling, and her energy is always cranked to 11. She thinks about music so much that she even talks in song lyrics. On the off-chance she doesn't have her guitar with her, everything can and will be turned into a musical instrument. You can always count on Luna to help out, and she'll do most anything you ask, as long as you're okay with her supplying a rocking guitar accompaniment.

LUAN LOUD
THE JOKESTER (14)

Luan's a standup comedienne who provides a nonstop barrage of silly puns. She's big on prop comedy too – squirting flowers and whoopee cushions – so you have to be on your toes whenever she's around. She loves to pull pranks and is a really good ventriloquist – she is often found doing bits with her dummy, Mr. Coconuts. Luan never lets anything get her down; to her, laughter IS the best medicine.

LYNN LOUD
THE ATHLETE (13)

Lynn is athletic and full of energy and is always looking for a teammate. With her, it's all sports all the time. She'll turn anything into a sport. Putting away eggs? Jump shot! Score! Cleaning up the eggs? Slap shot! Score! Lynn is very competitive, tends to be superstitious about her teams, and accepts almost any dare.

LUCY LOUD
THE EMO (8)

You can always count on Lucy to give the morbid point of view in any given situation. She is obsessed with all things spooky and dark – funerals, vampires, séances, and the like. She wears mostly black and writes moody poetry. She's usually quiet and keeps to herself. Lucy has a way of mysteriously appearing out of nowhere, and try as they might, her siblings never get used to this.

LANA LOUD
THE TOMBOY (6)

Lana is the rough-and-tumble sparkplug counterpart to her twin sister, Lola. She's all about reptiles, mud pies, and muffler repair. She's the resident Ms. Fix-it and is always ready to lend a hand – the dirtier the job, the better. Need your toilet unclogged? Snake fed? Back-zit popped? Lana's your gal. All she asks in return is a little A-B-C gum, or a handful of kibble (she often sneaks it from the dog bowl).

LOLA LOUD
THE BEAUTY QUEEN (6)

Lola could not be more different from her twin sister, Lana. She's a pageant powerhouse whose interests include glitter, photo shoots, and her own beautiful, beautiful face. But don't let her cute, gap-toothed smile fool you; underneath all the sugar and spice lurks a Machiavellian mastermind. Whatever Lola wants, Lola gets – or else. She's the eyes and ears of the household and never resists an opportunity to tattle on trouble-makers. But if you stay on Lola's good side, you've got yourself a fierce ally – and a lifetime supply of free makeovers.

LISA LOUD
THE GENIUS (4)

Lisa is smarter than the rest of her siblings combined. She'll most likely be a rocket scientist, or a brain surgeon, or an evil genius who takes over the world. Lisa spends most of her time working in her lab (the family has gotten used to the explosions), and says her research leaves little time for frivolous human pursuits like "playing" or "getting haircuts." That said, she's always there to help with a homework question, or to explain why the sky is blue, or to point out the structural flaws in someone's pillow fort. Lisa says it's the least she can do for her favorite test subjects, er, siblings.

LILY LOUD
THE BABY (15 MONTHS)

Lily is a giggly, drooly, diaper-ditching free spirit, affectionately known as "the poop machine." You can't keep a nappy on this kid – she's like a teething Houdini. But even when Lily's running wild, dropping rancid diaper bombs, or drooling all over the remote, she always brings a smile to everyone's face (and a clothespin to their nose). Lily is everyone's favorite little buddy, and the whole family loves her unconditionally.

CLYDE McBRIDE
THE BEST FRIEND (11)

Clyde is Lincoln's partner in crime. He's always willing to go along with Lincoln's crazy schemes (even if he sees the flaws in them up front). Lincoln and Clyde are two peas in a pod and share pretty much all of the same tastes in movies, comics, TV shows, toys – you name it. As an only child, Clyde envies Lincoln – how cool would it be to always have siblings around to talk to? But since Clyde spends so much time at the Loud household, he's almost an honorary sibling anyway. He also has a major crush on Lori.

HAROLD McBRIDE
CLYDE'S DAD

Harold, one of Clyde's Dads, is a level-headed straight-shooter with a heart of gold. The more easygoing of Clyde's dads, Harold often has to convince Howard that it's okay for them to not constantly hover over Clyde. Harold also has an athletic side – he played baseball in college and he and Howard are always up for challenging themselves physically, going as far as to take part in the Royal Woods Samurai Warrior competition.

HOWARD McBRIDE
CLYDE'S OTHER DAD

Howard, Clyde's other Dad, is a constantly anxious helicopter parent. Howard is emotional, whether it be sad times (like when Clyde stubbed his toe) or happy (like when Clyde and Lincoln beat that really tough video game). Howard is endlessly supportive of Clyde and is always by his side (watching to make sure nothing goes wrong). When he's not watching Clyde's every move, he's taking care of the McBrides' cats, Cleopawtra and Nepurrtiti or playing the jazz saxophone.

LYNN LOUD SR.

Dad (Lynn Loud Sr.) is a fun-loving, upbeat aspiring chef. A kid-at-heart, he's not above taking part in the kids' zany schemes. In addition to cooking, Dad loves his van, playing the cowbell and making puns. Before meeting Mom, Dad spent a semester in England and has been obsessed with British culture ever since – and sometimes "accidentally" slips into a British accent. When Dad's not wrangling the kids, he's pursuing his dream of opening his own restaurant where he hopes to make his "Lynn-sagnas" world famous.

RITA LOUD

Mother to the eleven Loud kids, Mom (Rita Loud) wears many different hats. She's a chauffeur, homework-checker and barf-cleaner-upper all rolled into one. She's always there for her kids and ready to jump into action during a crisis, whether it's a fight between the twins or Leni's missing shoe. When she's not chasing the kids around or at her day job as a dental hygienist, Mom pursues her passion: writing. She also loves taking on house projects and is very handy with tools (guess that's where Lana gets it from). Between writing, working and being a mom, her days are always hectic but she wouldn't have it any other way.

BOBBY SANTIAGO
LORI'S BOYFRIEND (17)

Bobby is sweet, a little dense, and just as obsessed with Lori as she is with him. He's a romantic who considers each new week with Lori an anniversary worth celebrating. He's on the phone with her constantly and will do anything for her. He's a man of many jobs, including but not limited to pizza delivery boy, pool lifeguard, mall security guard, and grocery stock boy.

INTRODUCTION

What is family?

Growing up as number 9 of 10 kids — to me, that was family.

My best friend had only one sibling. That was family to him.

Families come in all shapes and sizes and are more diverse today than ever before. My kids have friends who have two dads, friends who have two moms. Some friends have only one mom or one dad. Some friends live with their grandparents and some are blended by race and even religion. All of these are families and like with all families, there are good times and bad times and everything in between.

I hope to convey it all and represent it all in *THE LOUD HOUSE*. And if you watch the show or read these comics, I hope you see that *THE LOUD HOUSE* is about fun, *THE LOUD HOUSE* is about love, *THE LOUD HOUSE* is about acceptance, but most importantly, *THE LOUD HOUSE* is about family.

Enjoy!
Chris Savino
Creator of The Loud House

"BACK TO SCHOOL SHOPPING"

NO, THESE ARE NOT ALL FOR ME. TODAY I'M TRAPPED AT THE MALL WITH MY SISTERS FOR OUR--

--ANNUAL BACK-TO-SCHOOL SHOPPING TRIP.

IT'S THE LONGEST DAY OF MY LIFE.

"THEY HAVE TO GO TO EVERY SINGLE STORE IN THE MALL AND TRY EVERY SINGLE THING ON."

BUT DO THEY BUY ANYTHING?

"NOT UNLESS EVERY SINGLE ONE OF THEM SIGNS OFF ON THE PURCHASE."

KHAKI'S YOUR COLOR, NOT DENIM!

BUT THAT'S NOT THE WORST PART...

"THEY TRY TO DRESS ME..."

NO, NO, NO!

OKAY, OKAY, BUT JUST TRY THIS ON!

MAYBE I'LL JUST HIDE BEHIND THESE BAGS FOR THE NEXT FOUR HOURS...

LINCOLN! COME ON! WE'RE GOING SHOE SHOPPING NEXT!

THEY'VE GOT CLOGS IN YOUR SIZE!

I'M NOT WEARING CLOGS!

I GOTTA GET OUT OF HERE!

"POPSICLE PROBLEMS"

NEW GROCERIES MEANS A FRESH BOX OF POPSICLES!

AND GETTING HERE MEANS I GET THE ONE AND ONLY GRAPE!

I CALL DIBS ON GRAPE!

NUH-UH, IT'S MINE!

I LITERALLY, SMELL NEW POPSICLES.

UH-OH!

DUDES, I FOUND SNEAKER PRINTS!

THE GRAPE IS GONE!

I SMELL LINCOLN!

TIME TO HIDE!

GET THE GRAPE!

14

"HOPPILY EVER AFTER"

"DATE NIGHT"

I'LL BE THERE IN FIVE!

GREAT! I'LL MEET YOU OUTSIDE. I JUST GOTTA GET PAST MY *YOU-KNOW-WHATS* WHO WILL WANT TO TAG ALONG...

YOUR *PARENTS* WANT TO COME ON OUR DATE? THAT'S COOL, BABE!

OOOOOOOOHHHHH

CRASH BANG

I WAS TALKING ABOUT MY *SIBLINGS*...

TIME TO USE MY BAG OF TRICKS.

A THREE-HOLED BUTTON?! WHAT A FIND!

≷SNIFF≷ ≷SNIFF≷ I SMELL LORI'S PERFUME! IS SHE GOING ON A DATE?

"THE SNEEZE!"

CLYDE, WHY ARE WE HIDING IN THE ATTIC?

IN THE DARK?

BECAUSE, DADS, WE HAVE TO TAKE THE CATS TO THE VET TODAY AND I DON'T WANT THEM TO HEAR US.

~CLICK~

ALREADY? BUT I HAVEN'T HEALED FROM THEIR LAST VISIT!

WE JUST HAVE TO GET *CLEOPAWTRA* AND *NEPURTITTI* IN THESE CAGES.

STAY CALM; THEY CAN SMELL FEAR.

OH, KIIIIITTY CATS!

THEY'RE ONTO US! THEY'RE IN THE WIND!

FOUND ONE!

"LAND ESCAPE"

"HOUSE TRAINING"

"TROPICAL PARADISE"

"TIRED OUT"

END

36

"LIGHTS OUT"

"THE 10-HEADED BEAST"

LINC, THE WHITE-HAIRED BARBARIAN, SLOWLY MAKES HIS WAY THROUGH THE HAUNTED WOODS WHERE CERTAIN DOOM LURKS BEHIND EVERY CORNER AND UNDER EVERY CUSHION...

AYE, I MUST NOT ALERT ANY EVIL THAT SURELY INHABITS THESE LANDS.

LIIINCOOLN!

NO!

THE TALES ARE TRUE!

IT'S WHAT I FEARED MOST--

THE 10-HEADED BEAST!

OH EM GOSH! SO *RUDE!*

≈SIGH≈ WATCH OUT, LINCOLN.

POO POO!

I MUST STAND MY GROUND AND FIGHT THIS FOUL MONSTER!

MOM! LINCOLN IS COSPLAYING IN HIS UNDERWEAR AGAIN!

END

"TRAFFIC JAM"

"BAGGED AND BOARDED"

REALLY, REALLY LATER THAT EVENING...

"FINALLY!"

HOME, SWEET HOME. AND IN ONE PIECE TOO!

AFTER A LONG DAY OF AVOIDING POTENTIAL DISASTER, TIME TO READ SOME COMICS!

FIRST, TO CAREFULLY REMOVE THE COMIC FROM THE BAG...

AND THEN CAUTIOUSLY OPEN THE FIRST PAGE...

RIIIIP

DANG IT!

END

"SHOE STYLIN'"

45

47

"THE ART OF COOKING"

THERE'RE A LOT OF MOUTHS TO FEED IN THE LOUD FAMILY, BUT YOU'LL HEAR NO COMPLAINTS FROM ME, BECAUSE I HAPPEN TO *LOVE* COOKING!

AND TONIGHT, I'LL SHOW YOU HOW TO COOK ONE OF OUR FAVORITE FAMILY MEALS--

ENCHILADA CASSEROLE!

FIRST THINGS FIRST, GATHER YOUR INGREDIENTS!

HRMM...MISSING A FEW THINGS HERE IN THE PANTRY. NO DRIED CHILIS OR TOMATO SAUCE...

NO WORRIES! THIS CREAM OF PINEAPPLE WILL GIVE US BOTH THAT SWEETNESS AND TEXTURE WE NEED!

NOW ONTO STEP TWO. SIMMER IN A POT TO MAKE THE SAUCE!

AND A QUICK TASTE TEST TO SEE HOW WE'RE DOING...

PFEFFT

BLECH!

STEP THREE, ADD MORE SALT.

51

"THE BORROWERS"

YOU MAY BE WONDERING WHY I'M LOCKING UP MY MOST PRIZED POSSESSIONS.

WELL, MY SISTERS LIKE TO BORROW MY THINGS FROM TIME TO TIME.

"IT STARTS OUT INNOCENTLY...

MAY I BORROW THESE JEANS?

"BUT THEY DON'T EXACTLY RETURN THEM IN THE BEST SHAPE..."

OOPSIE!

BOOT

"SOMETIMES IT HAPPENS SO FAST...

HOPS NEEDS A PARTNER FOR SWING DANCING... MAY I BORROW THIS?

"...BEFORE I CAN EVEN RESPOND...

SLURP

"...THE DAMAGE IS DONE."

"I NEVER KNOW WHEN IT'LL HAPPEN NEXT..."

HEY, MAY I BORROW YOUR PHONE?

THANKS, BYE

LORI! YOU GOT YOUR MAKE-UP ALL OVER IT!

3:04 PM

AND YOU CHANGED MY BACKGROUND?!

THAT'S WHY I INVESTED IN THIS BABY! TO KEEP ALL MY STUFF SAFE FROM MY SISTERS.

HELLO, BIG BROTHER. MAY I BORROW SOME SOCKS? NOT TO WEAR...FOR AN EXPERIMENT.

SORRY, LIS, THE BANK OF LINCOLN LOUD IS CLOSED.

PAT PAT

I NEED TO BORROW A PEN...AND DAD'S CHECKBOOK, IF YOU HAVE THAT, TOO.

NO AND NO.

UNLESS YOU CAN CRACK THE CODE ON THIS BABY.

PAT PAT

END

MUSCLE FISH

HALF FISH. ALL MUSCLE. MERCURY CITY'S VIGILANTE SCOURS THE STREETS FOR EVILDOERS. BECAUSE THAT'S HOW HE ROLLS...

TONIGHT LOOKS LIKE A GOOD NIGHT TO...

'THOOM

...SCHOOL SOME FISH!

DON'T YOU BE KO! WITH US, TUNA-MELT!

SUSHI STRIKE FORCE... ATTACK!

MUSCLE-UP, BUTTERCUPS. NO MORE MR. RICE GUY.

58

WATCH OUT FOR PAPERCUTZ

Welcome to the second, sister-saturated *THE LOUD HOUSE* graphic novel from Papercutz—those sometime squabbling comicbook-lovers dedicated to publishing great graphic novels for all ages. I'm Jim Salicrup, the Editor-in-Chief and big-time ACE SAVVY fan, and I'm here to talk about how people actually read comics.

READING COMICS ALL AFTERNOON -- THE PERFECT SATURDAY!

UH-OH! TOO MANY JUICE BOXES!

In the episode "Undie Pressure," it's revealed that Lincoln Loud enjoys reading his comics wearing only his underpants, much to the dismay of his sisters. That got us to thinking about how people read their comics and graphic novels.

Jeff Whitman, editor of *THE LOUD HOUSE* graphic novels, enjoys reading comics on a couch, on his hour-long subway ride home, and in the park, where it's particularly peaceful.

Michelle Hart, our Marketing Coordinator, tends to get her comics digitally. She especially enjoys being able to enlarge comics lettering on her screen for her sore eyes. Her favorite places to read comics are either in bed or on the back porch.

When I was a kid, I read comics in bed too. I would lay tummy-down on my old iron folding bed with my head hanging out over the top and my mouth resting on part of the flat metal bedframe, while the comic was on the floor or in my hands. This actually pushed back my front teeth—it was as if I wore braces to make my teeth crooked!

Then there's how we keep our comics once we're done reading them. Lincoln wants to keep his prized comics in perfect condition, and goes to great lengths to preserve his comic in "Bagged and Boarded," only to be ultimately frustrated. I can relate! Other kids might just roll up their comics and keep them in their back pockets. What do you like to do with yours?

However you like to read and keep your comics, the important thing is that you enjoy them, especially those published by Papercutz, such as *BREADWINNERS, HARVEY BEAKS, NICKELODEON PANDEMONIUM!, PIG GOAT BANANA CRICKET* (check out the preview on the following pages!), and of course, *THE LOUD HOUSE!* Don't miss Volume 3, coming soon—and feel free to enjoy it any way you like!

Thanks,

JIM

THE HERO

STAY IN TOUCH!

EMAIL: salicrup@papercutz.com
WEB: papercutz.com
TWITTER: @papercutzgn
INSTAGRAM: @papercutzgn
FACEBOOK: PAPERCUTZGRAPHICNOVELS
FANMAIL: Papercutz, 160 Broadway, Suite 700, East Wing, New York, NY 10038

PIG, STARS ARE *EXPLODING* BALLS OF GAS THAT ARE HELD TOGETHER BY THEIR OWN GRAVITY! THAT ONE IS CALLED *ALNILAM*, AND IT IS 375,000 TIMES BRIGHTER THAN *THE SUN!*

WHOA! THAT'S *AWESOME.*

NO WAY, DUDE! THAT'S NOT SOME DUMB GAS BALL, IT'S ORION'S BELT BUCKLE!

"ORION"?

YEAH, DUDE! HE'S THIS ANCIENT GREEK *SUPERHERO* WHO COULD WALK ON WATER AND HAD THE POWER TO *TAME* ANY BEAST. HE *RULED* SO HARD, ZEUS TURNED HIM INTO STARS WHEN HE KICKED THE BUCKET.

THAT'S RIDICULOUS!

IF YOU'RE SO SURE IT'S NOT ORION, THEN WHY DON'T YOU GO PROVE IT?

MAYBE.

I.

WILL!

OH, BROTHER.

To be concluded in NICKELODEON PANDEMONIUM! #3!

THE CASAGRANDE FAMILY IS ABOUT TO GET LOUD